The Girl Who Found the Magic

Donovan Chin

United Writers Press
Asheville, N.C.
2024

ISBN: 978-1-952248-50-4

Published by:

United Writers Press
Asheville, NC 28803

Printed in the USA.

To my grandmother

Ivy Louise Beckford

the woman who is the sole maker of the foundation on which I stand.

AUTHOR'S NOTE

My main intention in writing this book is to challenge its readers to pay close attention to their thoughts and imaginations.

"As a man thinks, so is he," does not work sometimes. It works *all* the time. We cannot change our present circumstances. They are the reactions from our past actions, thoughts, and imaginations—conscious and unconscious. We have something far greater than our present circumstances. We are blessed with the power of thought, to think whatever we want in any circumstance, anytime.

It is our greatest gift from God.

I want you to see the good in everything and be grateful, no matter what your present life situation is because if you could hear what other people are enduring on this planet you would smile and be thankful.

No matter what you are going through, the fact that you still have a working brain is all the reason to feel good. We cannot see what's coming towards us but we have the ability to deal with anything—if we control our minds.

If you got turned down from a once-in-a-lifetime job, where you could make a million dollars per year, you would feel disappointed and think you have no luck. But suppose something happened a week later and everyone died in the building where your office would have been?

Your thoughts would change. You would probably feel lucky that you were not chosen for the job.

I hope you get my point. If you pay close attention to the girl in this story I am sure this book will be a tool to help you live a happy and fulfilled life.

Thank you and enjoy the experience.

Life is beautiful—you just have to find the beauty in it.

Donovan Chin

The Girl Who Found the Magic

ONE

Valery was born in New York, and lived in the Bronx with her parents, Yvette and Linton Bartley. Yvette and Linton were from the beautiful Caribbean island of Jamaica, a place she longed to visit. She had often begged her parents to take a vacation there because they had never been back since her birth, and she was now seven years old.

The Bartleys were not folks of great means, but to the onlooker, you would never know it because of how they lived their life and the image they portrayed. One would never know that the Bartleys sometimes struggled with their finances in order to make Valery's life as "normal" as possible. They wanted Valery to have a childhood filled with her own pleasant memories—memories she could call upon and share with her own family one day.

During summer months, there were visits to the zoo, circus, aquarium, movies, the Botanical Gardens, cookouts with family and friends. Valery was enrolled in dance classes. She learned to play the piano. If there was an activity that Valery's parents thought a sacrifice could be made to benefit their daughter, they made it happen. It helped that she was an only child.

Although Valery never visited Jamaica, there was no shortage of Jamaican culture in her upbringing. She had eaten all the Jamaican foods anyone could imagine but what she enjoyed most was eating her favorite fruit, the Julie mango with its sweet, delicious unique flavor and texture.

Valery also heard many Jamaican folktales handed down from generation to generation, like Bredda Ananci, Rolling Calves, Big Boy, Ol'Hige, and many more. At times, she sat quietly and listened to her parents reminiscing on their childhoods, which they often did. These story time moments were not just for entertainment purposes but also teachable opportunities for Valery. They wanted to give Valery an insight into their upbringing and the Jamaican way of life. They wanted most of all to share the memories they carried around with them—memories they brought back from their own childhoods during the fifties, sixties, and seventies.

The Bartleys had grown up in central Jamaica in the parish of Clarendon. The town where they lived was Chapelton, in the district of Sangster's Heights, a government housing scheme named after a late Jamaican prime minister.

Valery's parents would talk about going to the river to do laundry with their parents. Washing clothes down at the river was almost like going on a family outing because other parents had their children with them as well. Washday was one of the few times when all the children could get together to play with each other.

It was more fun for the children than the adults for obvious reasons. The children played on the riverbanks or splashed about in the shallow parts of the river. Over time, most of them would venture out and teach themselves how to swim. There was always one or more adults watching them as their parents toiled away.

The little washday community bustled with folks preparing lunch. Zinc pans bubbled over with dumplings, yam, and cassava on open, blazing fire pits.

You cannot have boiled dumplings, yam, and cassava without ackee and saltfish; that was a must-have on washday down by the river. Men caught fish and shrimp to sweeten the lunch pot. Some men climbed breadfruit trees, selected the proper ones for roasting, while others collected firewood and dry bamboo to keep the firepit ablaze.

A familiar topic of conversation was about how some of the bigger boys and girls were very carefree in their ways of finding provisions to add to the lunch pot. They would often return with their arms filled with ears of corn, stolen from farms that were nearby. Upon their return, and as they approached the fire pit, they would pick up speed—trying to be the first to unload their goods. In their haste, they usually spilled some, causing the men much laughter as the children scramble to pick up their spill.

Looking back on those long decades brought back the most incredible nostalgia, but there was a newness in the air in those days. Life was simple yet full of meaning. Living in the 2000s was life somewhere in the distant future that no one back then could have imagined. But time advanced and it became a different world.

Valery often thought to herself about her parents' stories. Even though those days sounded like fun, it would be terrible to live without a cell phone, a fridge, or a computer. Can you imagine, thinking of electricity as a luxury? "Mommy, Daddy, I am so glad I was born in these modern times," she would say. "If I needed water, I would have to walk for miles through the woods to the river. Wow! I can't imagine that."

One lovely spring evening, Valery was in her room preparing to start her homework while Mrs. Bartley was busy preparing dinner. She pushed her chair close to the bed and laid her math book on the bed, which she used as her desk. The book was open to the page where her homework was. She heaved a deep sigh as she pondered how to begin solving the problems.

Valery had a hard time solving algebra problems. "If only I was smarter, I could do these math problems in no time," she thought. "Man, I hate mathematics."

Wishing away her math homework, she closed her eyes and laid her head on the bed with her chest resting on top of the textbook. Her mind wandered until she was somewhere far away, at her parents' childhood homes. Her imagination took flight and she found herself in Jamaica.

She looked around excited, her eyes wide open. She paused in the middle of a deep breath and was unable to exhale. Speechless, she looked around at sights near and far.

"Wow, this must be the place," she thought. It was beautiful, with wildflowers all around, big trees with pretty blossoms, other trees with ripe fruits, oranges, June plums, guavas, mangoes, tamarinds, guineps, coconuts, bananas, star apples.

She saw the colorful birds her parents had spoken of and heard them chirping. Their many different melodious sounds were like an orchestra of a million pieces. Not too far away, she could hear and see the river. As the water made its way through the rocks and stones, it sounded like the steady applause of one hundred thousand hands. Her mouth shifted to a smile from ear to ear and her eyes sparkled with delight.

Valery turned completely around. She was alone. Despite all the beauty around, she was terrified. She wanted to run but thought to herself, "Where would I run to?" Tears welled up and rolled down her cheeks. "I want to go home," she whimpered. "I want my mommy and daddy." Fear took over and she shouted in the biggest voice she could muster, "Help, somebody! Please, help me! Help me!"

From out of nowhere, a tall, elegant, chocolate-skinned woman appeared wearing a bandana dress and matching head tie. Her lips were red like ripe tomatoes, and she wore earrings to match in color. A colorful necklace adorned her throat and glittering bracelets were on both her wrists.

The frightened girl looked with wonder and excitement at the lovely woman who appeared before her. She no longer felt alone—she was more curious to learn who this woman was who appeared like magic.

The woman's red lips seem to move in slow motion as they stretched to form a smile that gave way to snow-white teeth that lit up her attractive face. It was as if the night was giving way to the morning sun. Valery felt an increased sense of security.

"My lovely little girl, what is the reason for your tears?" the woman asked.

"I want my parents. I want to go home. Where am I really?" responded Valery.

"No need to worry, my dear child, your mom and dad are just fine."

"Do you know my parents? Have you seen them? How do you know they are fine?"

Not wanting to lose the curiosity she saw on Valery's face she said, "I see that you are in your inner world, a place where you have come to find magic."

A puzzled look crept over Valery's face. "Magic, what magic? I am not looking for any magic, I want to go home." Tears rolling down her face again, she wiped her face with the back of her hand. "Can you help me, please?"

Looking deeply into the dark mysterious eyes of the woman, Valery felt as if she was falling effortlessly into the arms of the woman with the dark eyes and pretty smile. The woman knelt and hugged her gently but firmly and said with a soft assuring voice, "I am here to help you. Don't you worry, my child. I am the servant of your imagination."

Valery looked at her without understanding but the woman continued. "If you don't have a clear picture in your mind, I will not get a clear command so you must help me to help you. Think of me as the genie of your mind."

Clear picture, and clear command...what does that mean? If she wanted to go home, Valery decided, she must learn more about the stranger and how she might help her to get home. She dried her eyes. "I am thankful that you are here with me in this strange but beautiful place. What is your name? Where are you from?" The woman released her arms from around the girl and took a seat under a big mango tree. She guided Valery to sit on her lap and they both sat for a while and took in the beauty around them.

Pretty birds of all colors and sizes chirped melodies Valery could close her eyes and relax quite easily to. Smaller birds flew in and out of trees, flitting about from branch to branch. Butterflies in all their intricately designed glory fluttered from flower to flower, paused to show off the handiwork that only Mother Nature herself could paint on the canvas of a butterfly's wing. Bumblebees busily collected pollen from flowers and blossoms from shrubs and big trees.

The sweet smell of freshness wafted through the air. The wind carried different fragrances displaying the personality of each variety of plants. Valery opened her eyes and looked around. A sea of lavender perfumed the air with dominance.

The woman said, "I am the servant of your imagination, and you can call me your Auntie Genie." She paused before continuing. "You see, my child, you live in two worlds. The place where you are right now is your imaginary world and it is from this imaginary world that you can create a completely new world. The outer world is where you, your friends, and your family reside—along with all material things."

"Wow! How did I get here?"

Auntie Genie smiled. "You came here because of your fear of mathematics. You tried so hard to avoid facing your fear that you imagined you were in Jamaica and through the strength of your imagination, I, the servant of your mind, must grant you your wish."

"You mean I can imagine anything, really? Anything I want I can make it happen. Wow! But…but how?"

The woman answered, "My child you can have, be, or do anything you can imagine. Light bulbs came from someone's imagination. Who thought such a creative thing was possible? Computers, televisions, cell phones—all came by way of people's creativity. Just think what the world would be like without the power of imagination and the ability to create in your mind." They held hands like mother and daughter as they strolled to a nearby river. "Everyone has this power to have, be, or do anything. To use this power, you must learn to focus your heart and mind."

The branches of a lime tree hung over the river. The woman picked a lime and showed it to Valery. "Close your eyes and imagine eating this lime. How does your mouth feel? What sensations are coming forth? As you imagine different things, your mouth will feel different."

Valery began to feel the sourness in her mouth. "It's true, Auntie Genie, I tried it and it worked. My mouth felt as though I had tasted the lime."

Valery looked at the surface of the water and saw her reflection and took notice that even though water was flowing down the stream her reflection did not move. Curious to know why the water did not carry her reflection away, Valery asked Auntie Genie. The woman responded with an answer more philosophical than scientific. She explained how everyone's life is a reflection of their mind.

"What you mean by that?"

"What you choose to put into your mind, whether positive or negative influences, represents the flowing water. Your reflection is the life you carved out based on how you chose to use your mind."

"So, will my positive imagination help me to find my way home?"

"My child, your imagination can take you anywhere!"

"Wow!"

They came to a footpath and stopped. Auntie Genie smiled softly at Valery.

"My dear, it's time to find your way home. Remember everything I told you."

"Yes, Auntie, thank you so much." The woman raised her right hand and pointed her finger in the direction Valery should go.

"Remember, my dear child, do not look for the easy way. There are no free rides. There is always a hidden cost to pay." Valery, hesitating, took a few steps, looked back, and waved at the woman. She turned and looked back again, and the mysterious woman was gone.

Valery wondered where she could have gone so quickly. Auntie Genie's disappearance frightened her a bit. She turned and started running as fast as she could. She ran and walked and walked and ran. Valery had been on her journey for what seemed like hours, and she was beginning to get tired and thirsty.

In the distance, she could hear running water and the thought of quenching her thirst quickened her steps. Valery followed the sound until a little spring came into view. Water gushed from a rock as it poured its contents down into a clear pool below and over rocks to form small waterfalls.

The flow of water meandered through the woods and out of sight. Valery turned her gaze back to where the water was exiting the big rock. Rose apple trees grew alongside the stream, cascading their lovely fruiting branches low enough to pick their sweet, delicious fruit. Tired as the day was long, she knelt, cupped her hands, and drank until she was satisfied. Then she picked a few apples and devoured those as well.

Weary from the journey, she slumped down on the ground, closed her eyes, and rested for a while. When she opened her eyes again, she looked up to see a robin perched on an overhanging rose apple branch looking right at her as if to say, "I see you and I know you have come a long way." She smiled at the bird, waved, then off she went running again.

She continued through the woods and climbed a not-so-steep hill, the top of which opened to a meadow. From where she stood, she could hear the rumbling sounds of vehicles traveling but could not see them because of the tall grass. Unable to contain her excitement, Valery quickly made her way down through the meadow only to find there was a small patch of guava trees she had to navigate before the main road came into view.

Valery arrived breathless. Gasping for air, she bent over with both hands on her knees. Even so, she could not escape the beauty around her. She looked up and down the street, gazing at the beautiful wildflowers growing along the roadsides. Having caught her breath, she stood up and looked to her right and left, wondering which way to go. *Auntie Genie did not tell me where to go when I got to the main road. She just said to follow my heart.*

Her thoughts were interrupted by a sudden loss of light. Dark clouds began to steal away the glow of the sun. Flashes of lightning and rolling thunder would soon give way to heavy rain. The frightened child was desperate because the weather would soon change, and she had nowhere to shelter. Tears flowed down Valery's cheeks as the rain started to drizzle. She ran to a nearby plum tree that stood close to the road and was heavily laden with foliage.

Out of nowhere, a red car like no car she had ever seen came around the corner and stopped right by the tree. She could see two children in the backseat of the car. The car door opened. A bright red umbrella made its exit out the door followed by a woman wearing a red pantsuit with white gloves and a cute white hat.

"Oh you pretty little girl, what are you doing here all by yourself?" she asked. She held out her hand to Valery and added, "Come let me take you home. What is your name?"

"My name is Valery. I am lost. I want to go home to my parents."

"Don't worry, my dear. I will take you home." The woman helped Valery in the backseat and drove off just as the clouds burst open and more rain came tumbling down.

After what seemed like endless driving through winding mountain roads and crossing many bridges, the car finally drove up to a very big gate and stopped. Valery felt confused. "Where are we? This is not my home."

The woman smiled. "I know but it's getting late. You can rest here overnight, and I will make sure you get home tomorrow." Valery once again expressed her gratitude.

During the ride, she was so excited at the prospect of finally going home that she never spoke to the woman except to tell her where she lived. "Excuse me," she said. "What is *your* name?"

"I am Madam Consequence," she said, "but you can just call me Madam."

The big gate slowly opened, and they drove down a long driveway. The car stopped at the top of the circular driveway in front of the house. Madam got out and escorted all three children through the largest set of front doors that Valery had ever seen.

TWO

The next morning, Valery was awakened by the sound of children playing outside. She stared at a big clock on the wall. It was ten o'clock. She jumped up, surprised that she had slept so long and that the madam did not come to take her home. She remembered going to a second-floor bedroom with lots of windows. Now that it was daylight, she could see what was beyond the wall of glass.

Peering out the window, she could see children playing in the yard on a well-manicured lawn. She could also see a long driveway lined with beautiful flowers on both sides leading all the way to the top of the circle in front of the house. Inside the circle was a lovely rose garden. Valery had never seen so many different colors of roses before. She smiled and tried to count the colors. There were red, white, pink, purple, orange, and yellow, with ferns in between them. It looked like someone had delivered a giant bouquet from a flower shop.

A bell rang, interrupting the children's playtime. No one lagged as they all hurried inside on cue. "Oh, this must be a private school," thought Valery. Just before she walked away from the window, she saw several elderly women and men walking towards the lawn. As soon as they walked on the grass, they branched off in different directions, each of them seeming tasked to do different things. Some picked up after the children and some took care of the garden. She also noticed something strange—no one spoke, no one acknowledged each other.

She hurried to the door and grabbed the doorknob. She pulled but the door did not open. She banged on it; no one came. She banged harder and harder, but to no avail.

Why is the door locked? Am I a prisoner? She certainly could not have left on her own. Where would she go?

Fearing that something was amiss, Valery was determined to get someone's attention. She yelled, kicked, and banged on the door with all her strength. "Let me out, let me out, please, please, somebody let me out of here. I want to go home! Help! Help!" Fear and anger got the better of her, and she screamed like a wild banshee.

Finally, she heard loud footsteps coming down the long hallway toward the door. She stopped hitting the door and became quiet, holding her ear to it. As soon as she heard the footsteps stop directly outside the door, she stepped back. Keys jangled and then she heard a key inserted in the lock.

Valery stepped backward toward the window and the door swung open. A massive woman—larger than anyone Valery had ever seen stood in the doorway. What was she to do? Valery's eyes grew larger with every step the woman took toward her. Although now frightened out of her wits, she spoke up. "Where is the madam? I want to go home."

"Listen, you loudmouth," said the woman. "I want you to stop this shouting and behave yourself at once or else."

"Where is the madam?" repeated Valery. "She promised to take me home to my parents. Where is she?"

The woman smirked. "This is your new home. Didn't you know?" Grinning, she continued. "My dear, this is the house of consequences."

Valery's anger got the better of her. She grabbed a small lamp from the night table by the bedside and smashed it on the floor. She pushed over the nightstand, grabbed the pillow, threw it down, and stomped on it. "Let me out! let me out!" she shouted.

The woman grabbed and tried to restrain her, but the child was in such a rage that she could not. Fumbling around with the whistle on her neck, the woman finally managed to blow several times to call for assistance. Two men came running, one of whom held ropes. The other caught one of Valery's kicking feet. "Tie her up," commanded the woman, holding Valery's hands behind her.

Just as the men finished tying Valery up, the madam glided into the room as if on a magic carpet. Everyone quickly stopped what they were doing and jumped to their feet. Valery laid helplessly on the floor with both hands and feet bound. The madam signaled for everyone else to leave the room except for the giant woman. "Get this room cleaned up," said the woman.

"Yes, Madam," said the large woman, and she left the room in a hurry.

Valery, still helpless on the floor, began to weep. "Madam, you promised to take me home. Why are these people treating me this way? What did I do? Madam, please, please, Madam, get me out of here. Take me home to my parents."

Madam walked over to the window and gazed upon the well-manicured lawn and beautiful flowers. Slowly, she turned to face Valery, eyes blazing. "You willingly came into my car. You willingly walked through the doors of this house."

Tears flowed down the girl's face, like water from the spring she drank from the day before. "But, Madam," she said, "you promised to take me home to my parents. I believed and trusted you. Please, I beg you, please take me home."

Madam said something that sounded familiar. "*I* am Madam *Consequence*. I must remain loyal to your actions. Everyone who comes to this house, like you, accepts a ride seeking an easy way to their destination—not realizing there is only one right way. Every other way has its own consequences." She paused and gazed at Valery. "You can walk out of here when you are ready. You can free yourself but remember, once you leave, you can never return."

Valery thought to herself, "That's okay—I never want to come back."

"You can play it safe and stay here," said the madam, "or you can leave and pay the consequences of your own determination. It is up to you."

"Madam, please untie me so I may leave."

Madam walked to the door and turned. "Your actions are the reason you are bound. And only your actions will untie you. This is the house of consequences." She disappeared into the hallway, locking the door behind her.

Valery could feel her heart pounding like a fist punching her chest from inside. She had no idea what to do. Thoughts whirled through her mind. *How was I to know that taking a ride from someone who presented themselves as being trustworthy would turn out to be to my detriment?* With some effort, Valery managed to get herself into a seated position. With a bit more maneuvering, she was able to stand up. If she hopped over to the window, someone might see her.

A robin, just like the one she had seen at the spring, sat on the window ledge as though it was looking inside the room. It was then that Valery remembered Auntie's words. "I will be with you always, but you will only see me when you think of me."

She turned her thoughts to Auntie Genie and, in a flash, just like Cinderella's magical fairy godmother, Auntie Genie appeared.

Valery was so glad she shouted with joy. "Auntie Genie, thanks for coming to rescue me from this horrible place. Please take me home as fast as you can."

"My dear child, you can free yourself. If you can honestly accept the fact that you are the cause of your situation—and hold yourself responsible for it—all you have to is imagine being free and you will be."

"Auntie, my feet and hands are tied. How am I to do that?"

"My child, think about your freedom and not your bondage. Never waste precious time thinking about what is impossible. Think of what you want to do. Use your imagination. It is your greatest power."

Valery closed her eyes, concentrated and imagined that she was free.

In the background, she heard a small voice. "Think, think, my child. You have the power to do all that you can imagine."

Valery imagined that she was strong and powerful. She imagined that she could take that horrible woman and her helpers and throw them as far away as possible in a place where no one could find them again. She imagined seeing her parents waiting for her by a peaceful quiet stream—they were hugging and kissing her face all over.

She slowly opened her eyes and saw that her hands and feet were free! Her jaw dropped in astonishment. When she turned her palms up to look at them, she saw the movement in slow motion. When she kicked up her feet, they too were moving in slow motion. Was this really happening?

Astonishment quickly turned into joy and happiness. The excitement of what she witnessed temporarily robbed her of speech and breath. Then, with a sudden gasp for air, she heard words come out of her mouth. "Auntie Genie!! You did it! Thank you so, so much. I love you with all my heart. I knew you could do it!"

"Valery, my darling child, you did it all by yourself. You have found the magic. When thoughts, imagination, and feelings come together, you create magic."

Valery could not be happier. Her spirits were high, and she was overflowing with joy. "Wow, I can do magic. Wow!"

Auntie Genie turned Valery toward her and rested her hands on the girl's shoulders. Curiosity and adventure shone in the child's eyes.

"My little angel, you must go now. Go through that door and find your destiny. Go through the door and if you can open the gate, you will be free forever to have, be, or do whatever your little heart desires."

Valery walked up to the door and, as she reached for the handle, she remembered it was locked. She looked back at Auntie Genie, smiled with newfound confidence, and closing her eyes, imagined she gathered up a great puff of wind in her mouth and blew the door wide open. When she opened her eyes, the door banged against the wall. Was this for real?

As Valery left the room, she turned as if to look back at her fairy godmother. "Do not look back until you are where you want to be," said the all-knowing voice. "Go and find your destiny, use your imagination to create, and explore to your heart's content. Go now, my dear little angel."

Valery obeyed and continued down the long hallway—down the stairs, out the front door, and onto the driveway leading to the big gate. As she got closer to the entrance, she saw the massive ornate iron structure that stood before her. The gate looked more imposing than it had the night before. She looked at how high and how wide the gate was and wondered how she was going to get out. But she did not have to wonder long. Her lips parted into a big smile. She took a deep breath, exhaled slowly, relaxed her mind, gently closed her eyes, and imagined.

The big giant gate creaked as it slowly opened. Valery stepped through only to hear her mother calling her name. She was home!

"Your dinner is ready, pumpkin," said her mother. "Are you finished with your homework?"

Valery jumped up, ran to her mother, and threw her arms around her waist. She buried her face in her mother's stomach. "Oh, Mommy, I am so glad to see you."

Her mother looked at her, a curious expression on her face. "What is it? Is something wrong? Are you okay?"

"Yes, yes, I am fine," said Valery. "Where is Daddy?"

"He is working late tonight. He'll be home soon." Surprised at Valery's sudden outpouring of affection and interest in her father's whereabouts, Mrs. Bartley was a little worried but she quickly dismissed the girl's enthusiasm as a cause for concern. "Dinner is ready. Come eat," she said.

"Let me finish my studies," said Valery, as she started back to her room and her makeshift desk. "I will be right there. Thank you, Mom."

When she got to her room, she tackled her "wicked" math homework. Somehow, it seemed easier than before.

THREE

Valery went to school the following day, but as she was getting ready to leave at the end of the school day, her teacher approached her with a letter. "Please give this to your parents," she said.

"Thanks, Mrs. Anderson," she said. "Have a good evening." She put the letter in her bag and went home.

The letter was from the principal asking that one of her parents be present at school the next day. After Mrs. Bartley read the letter, she held the envelope to her lips and wondered what was happening to her daughter at school. She knew Valery was no troublemaker and, although she was not great in every subject, she knew her child was a good student.

Mrs. Anderson met with Valery and her mom the next morning. She walked them to the reception area outside the principal's office and told them to have a seat. Mrs. Anderson knocked once on the principal's door and without waiting for an answer, she let herself in and closed the door behind her. After a few minutes, Mrs. Anderson opened the door and beckoned for Valery and her mom to come into the office. She held the door open and as they walked through. "Principal Hornsby, this is Valery's mother, Mrs. Bartley."

The principal stood up. "Oh, yes, yes. Please have a seat."

Both Valery and her mother were still in the dark. The mood in the office was clearly not warm and fuzzy. Neither had a clue as to why they were there but they supposed everything would be made clear soon enough.

Mrs. Anderson stood beside the principal, who came straight to the point. "It has been brought to my attention that your child cheated on an exam yesterday. We do not and will not allow this kind of behavior in our school."

Mrs. Bartley, taken aback, turned to Valery. "Is this true?"

Valery was just as shocked as her mother and answered most emphatically, "No, Mommy, I swear…"

Mrs. Anderson interrupted her. She pulled Valery's exam from the folder she was holding. "Then how do you explain this?" Holding the paper in front of Valery, she continued. "You are the weakest child in my class when it comes to mathematics, and you are telling me you became a genius overnight? You are lying."

Mrs. Bartley was not about to stay quiet. "Wait one minute. You have no right speaking to my child—"

The principal interrupted her. "No need for this, we are only trying to rectify the situation before us."

"Why don't we let her take the exam again?" said Mrs. Anderson. "Right now."

Mrs. Bartley thought for a moment. If retaking the test would absolve her daughter of this ridiculous allegation then she did not have a problem with it. The principal wanted to satisfy any suspicion Mrs. Anderson had about cheating so he too thought retaking the test would resolve the issue. "Very well then," he said. "Would you like to take the test again right now?"

"Yes, sir," said Valery, shrugging. "I don't mind."

The principal cleared part of his desk, pulled up a chair, and instructed Valery to take a seat. Mrs. Anderson placed the exam on the table in front of the girl, gave her a pencil, and looked at the clock on the wall. "You may begin now," she said. She whispered to the principal that she had to get back to her class and would return in an hour. And with that, she walked out of the room.

After forty minutes, Valery placed her pencil on the desk. "I am finished, sir," she said.

The principal looked surprised and motioned for her to bring the paper to him. Once done matching her answers with the answer key Mrs. Anderson had provided, he took his glasses off and leaned back in his chair in disbelief.

"One moment," he said. He picked up his phone and dialed Mrs. Anderson on her cell. "Could you come to my office now, please?"

A few minutes later, Mrs. Anderson smugly entered the room, confident that Valery's deceit was out in the open for everyone to see. But to her surprise, Valery had not only finished but had answered all the questions correctly.

"I was right here," said Mr. Hornsby. "There was no way for her to cheat."

Mrs. Anderson was determined to prove that somehow Valery had had some form of aid to help her with the test. She offered another explanation.

"Maybe she memorized it."

"Memorized it? Come on, Mrs. Anderson, don't you think you are going overboard now?"

The teacher was so disappointed that the outcome was not what she had expected that she whispered to the principal, "Give her a test from a higher grade."

The principal was in total disagreement because Valery had proven that she understood the material and was able to take and pass the math test presented to her. Now he felt that Mrs. Anderson was behaving like a dog with a bone and was not going to leave the matter until she got her way. Eventually, he consented to the teacher's wish. If Valery took the test and did not do as well, he was not going to use it to penalize her because she would not have learned how to do the math from a higher grade yet, but he had no plans to reveal his thoughts to Mrs. Anderson.

Valery's mother, sensing that something was not quite right, spoke up. "What's going on?"

The principal said, "We are discussing the test. We think there might be a mistake so we would like her to retake a different test now—or she can come back tomorrow."

Mrs. Bartley looked at Valery. The girl smiled. "It's okay, Mommy."

"Well, then," said her mother, "since we are already here, we might as well get it over with. I need to know why this allegation came about in the first place."

The teacher left the room and returned with a new test. She placed it in front of Valery, smugly confident that the child would not be able to complete the test. She took a stopwatch from her pocket, pressed it, and said, "You may begin."

As before, after forty minutes, Valery put her pencil down. The principal looked at the teacher and back at the girl. "Finished? All of it?"

"Yes, sir," said Valery.

Mrs. Anderson shook her head in disgust. "You might be finished, but let's see how many are correct." She looked over the test in a hurry, comparing the answer key to Valery's answers. After a minute, she looked up, her face blanched. Valery had scored 100 percent again.

The principal's face was now red. "Mrs. Bartley, Valery, I am sorry we had to put you through this but when an accusation of this nature comes to my attention it is my responsibility as the principal of this school to investigate. I also want to add that in all my years as principal of this school, I have never seen anyone perform so brilliantly. If I had not witnessed it for myself, I would not have believed it." He turned to the girl. "Valery, I think your teacher has something to say to you both."

Mrs. Anderson nodded her head sheepishly.

"Valery, please forgive me. You have always been one of the weaker students in the class, so it was hard for me to think it was possible for you to suddenly do so well. You did even better than the best students in your mathematic class. I do not understand what has happened in such a short space of time to expand your comprehension about a subject you were struggling with, but no matter whatever miracle took place, I am not complaining. I am happy that the light came on and you are now able to connect the dots."

"I must confess, too," said Mrs. Bartley, "that I've noticed that something has changed for my daughter since a few days ago. It was as though she became a new person right before my very eyes."

After that day, Valery became the talk of the entire school. She was now the smartest child in her grade, which earned her a place among the crème de la crème of the accelerated learners. She received an award in recognition of her brilliance. At the award ceremony, she gave a very memorable speech, one that would lay the foundation for the rest of her life.

"At my young age, I have come to understand that everyone in this room and beyond can have, be or do anything they desire. The next thing I would like us to understand is that we are always creating, consciously or unconsciously. Our imagination is the tool we use to create our lives. Let me invite you to practice controlling your imagination, thereby controlling your lives. I think it's the most exciting thing any human being can ever do."

The crowd jumped to their feet, cheering and shouting. A familiar sight appeared on the podium—a beautiful robin, much like the one she had seen in her dream where she met Auntie Genie. The bird flew out the window as quickly as it appeared.

Valery smiled as the bird went away. "I love you, Auntie Genie," she whispered to herself.

FOUR

Years passed and Valery grew older. By the time she entered university in Atlanta, she was already a very popular speaker. Youth leaders from churches kept her number on speed-dial because she was a natural-born positive influencer for their young people. In their eyes, Valery had discovered the magical power of faith, which helped her to touch people and bring out the best in them.

After careful study, Valery came to realize that everyone has and uses faith in one way or another, but the question came down to, "What do we have faith in?"

Is it faith in the possibility that we will succeed in life or the belief that we might fail? The result of our faith depends on how strongly we believe in a positive or negative outcome, and whatever we have the most faith in will be ours—either good or bad.

Then, one day, Valery received a call from her mother asking her to come home immediately. An obedient child, she heeded her mother's request and boarded the first flight home. Her mom tried her best not to alarm her daughter but insisted that it was important for her to visit.

Valery guessed that something must have happened for her mother to summon her like that. She tried not to get excited or think what it could be because she did not want to get unnecessarily upset without knowing the reason.

When her taxi pulled up to the gate in front of her parents' house, her mom was already waiting patiently for her. Distress was written all over her face and she fought hard to hold back tears. Valery quickly paid the taxi driver, handing him a $100 bill, and grabbed her carry-on luggage. The taxi driver rolled down his window and shouted, "Hey, you are forgetting your change!"

Without looking back, Valery shouted, "It's okay, you can keep it!" She made a mad dash towards her mother, who was standing by the doorway.

The look on her mother's face was quite telling. It made Valery afraid and a sense of anxiety crept over her. In that instant, she knew in her gut that something had happened to her father. "Mom, where is Dad?"

Her mother did not know how to answer. All she could manage was open arms to embrace her daughter.

"Where is my father?" demanded Valery. She called out to him as she forced her way around her mother to get inside the house. As she burst through the door, she saw her Uncle Alfred, Auntie Sonia and some of her cousins— Jeffrey, Ann, Jessica, and Toni—but still no sign of her father.

"Where is Daddy?" Valery was beside herself now. "Somebody better say something or else I am going to continue shouting until I get answers."

Mrs. Bartley made her way through the door, walked up behind her, said as calmly as she could, "Baby, your father had a terrible accident."

Valery was stricken with fear. "Is he dead?"

Jessica, her favorite cousin, walked over and gave her a hug. "No, he is not dead. He is in the hospital."

"Where? Which hospital?" She turned to Jessica and said, "Please take me there."

Jessica's father, Valery's Uncle Alfred, took his car key from his pocket handed it to his daughter. "Here, use my car." The two hurried out of the house.

When they arrived at the hospital, they quickly made their way to the intensive care unit where Valery's father was. To their disappointment and frustration, the attending nurse told them that no one could enter the room for another hour because Mr. Bartley's doctor was making sure everything went well after his surgery.

Valery was not happy. She slumped her shoulders and hissed through her teeth as she walked away. Turning around, she asked the nurse where the waiting room was.

"Go down this hallway, at the end make a right, go to the end and make a left," she said. The two girls both walked in silence as they headed for the waiting room.

Jessica finally broke the silence. "Remember, they will come and get us when they are finished." Valery managed a weak smile.

They both took a seat, but no sooner had she sat down than Valery sprang up and paced the room. She stopped by the window to look at anything that might take her mind off her dad, if only for a few minutes. She thought of her roommate who she'd promised to keep posted. She was in no mood to talk, so she sent a text.

"My father had an accident. I am at the hospital waiting to see him. Will call you later." She pressed the send button, walked back to her seat, and sat down beside Jessica once again.

After another restless minute had gone by, Valery rose and walked into the hallway just in time to see a hospital worker approaching from down the hall and pushing an x-ray machine.

As the hospital worker was about to pass by with his machine in tow, he suddenly did a double take. "Valery! Valery, is that you?"

She looked at the handsome man. "Do you know me?"

The young man smiled. "How can I not know you? We were in the same class in high school. I can't believe you don't remember me. I'm Lambert DaCosta."

Valery came closer. "*My* Lambert DaCosta who used to bring fried-roast breadfruit for lunch?" She looked again at him. "Oh my gosh! Wow! How was I supposed to recognize you with all that hair on your face and moreover, what are you doing here? You are supposed to be out of state studying law."

Lambert sighed. "It's a long story. What are *you* doing here?"

"My dad had an accident."

"Oh," said Lambert, thinking, "you know I saw his name on a chart, but it did not ring a bell." He paused and looked around. "I could lose my job for telling you this, but he is still unconscious and they are saying even if he regains consciousness he will never walk again."

"What are you saying? No, no, no! That can't be true." Valery sobbed and Lambert cradled her to his chest and hugged her.

An announcement over the intercom called for the portable x-ray tech, stat. Lambert released Valery from his embrace. "That's me." He took a card from his pocket and gave it to Valery. "Call me if you need anything." He turned and dashed down the hall with the x-ray machine.

Valery tried to compose herself as she walked back to the waiting room. As soon as she entered the room, Jessica saw that she was crying and rushed towards her. "They said he may never walk again," said Valery, between sobs.

A nurse who looked to be in her mid-thirties approached them. She came to deliver news to the girls, but she saw how very upset they were and thought a few words of encouragement might help to lift their spirits.

This young nurse had her own sad story. She had lost her father to a drunk driving accident five years before she emigrated from Nigeria. "Everything will be okay," she said. "My dear sisters, God knows best. Maybe our life experiences are lessons to learn while we are here on this earth. Dry your tears, ladies. God is always in charge."

Then, remembering her mission, she paused. "Which one of you is Ms. Bartley?"

Valery nodded her head.

"You can see your father now. The doctor is waiting to answer any questions you may have."

Both Valery and Jessica grabbed their pocketbooks and hurried with the nurse, who escorted them to where

Valery's father was. The nurse introduced the girls to the doctor and he pulled the curtains back to reveal Mr. Bartley surrounded by machines and tubes and laying quietly in the bed.

"He is on life support right now," said the doctor. "We will just have to wait and see what happens."

Valery moved closer to the bed, pulled up a chair and sat clasping her father's right hand. Jessica stood behind her cousin, massaging her shoulders.

The doctor spoke again. "Is there anything you would like to know about your father's condition?"

Neither Valery nor Jessica could speak—all they could manage to do was shake their heads.

"If there is anything you would like to ask just have one of the nurses at the front desk page me."

The doctor turned to walk out of the room and Jessica turned to show their gratitude. "Thank you very much, Doctor. We appreciate everything you are doing."

Valery looked quite small as she sat hunched over her father's bedside. She stroked his hand affectionately. "Daddy, I am here," she said as tears ran down her cheeks. "You are going to be just fine." She reached over to cover her dad's feet and her phone fell from her lap.

As she bent down to reach under the bed for her phone, she caught a glimpse of something else under the bed. She grabbed her phone and then went around the bed.

"What is it?" said Jessica.

Valery bent down and retrieved a wallet. "It's Daddy's wallet. It must have fallen under the bed when they were putting his personal belongings away." Valery removed a picture from the wallet—a photo of her and her dad when she learned to ride a bike. She handed it to Jessica.

Jessica exclaimed. "Look at this! Oh, my word, this must have been eleven years ago. I remember you got the bike for your sixth birthday. Time really flies."

Valery smiled and continued to look through the wallet. She counted two hundred fifteen dollars and fifty cents and placed the cash in her own handbag for safekeeping.

FIVE

Three months passed. Mr. Bartley was still on life support and had shown no signs of improvement. Infighting among the family erupted because some felt it was time Mr. Bartley be released and go on to glory. Others, grounded in their spiritual beliefs, felt it was not yet time. They strongly believed that he would come around.

Valery told them, "There is no way Mom and I are going to let Dad down. We are going to pray him back into our lives. Just wait and see."

Valery and her mom decided that the family should meet at the hospital and hold a prayer vigil at Mr. Bartley's bedside. "If you have any doubt that prayers will work, please do not come. We want nothing but positive energy emanating from our beings."

The night before the prayer vigil, Valery could not sleep. She thought about her childhood encounter with her fairy godmother in the dream and tried to call upon her seven-year-old self and summon the woman back into her life.

"Auntie Genie," she said. "I know I am all grown up now, but you promised me that you would always be here for me. I still need you. Where are you? Please Auntie Genie, come and help my father."

When Valery finally fell asleep, Auntie Genie appeared in a dream. "My dear child, no one person is more alive than the next. A sick person is no closer to death than a healthy person. How many times have healthy people died before very sick people? No man can decide how long anyone should live. Circumstances can change any minute—especially if the person has enough will to live."

She paused. "Give your father a reason to live. Find a way, my child. Never visit a sick person with sadness and pity—the energy you carry to them can make them better or worse. See him as well in your mind and invite him back to good health."

When she woke, she promised herself that she would do her best to follow Auntie Genie's instructions.

Mrs. Bartley, Valery, Jessica, and her uncle were all present at the hospital—along with other members of the family who came to give extra strength and support. The hospital told the family only a few people could come in at a time. Mrs. Bartley nodded and took Valery's hand. Valery led the vigil. She poured her heart and soul into calling on the mercy and grace of Heaven upon her father lying motionless before the family. At the end, she told everyone to continue holding hands and instructed the family to recall their most positive and memorable moment with her dad. "Who will go first?"

After her uncle spoke, Valery went next. She dipped her hand in her pocket and took out the photo she'd found in her father's wallet. Everyone laughed as Valery told of her experience of riding a bike for the first time.

It was Mrs. Bartley's turn. She told of her most memorable moment with her husband. "He was there with me at the birth of our only child." She looked at Valery and smiled. "The doctor and everyone else were telling me to push and as I made that last push, I could feel the baby slowly leaving my body. I could not see what was happening, so I kept looking at my husband's face to tell me that she had fully arrived. The moment soon revealed itself when he let out a gasp and a big smile slowly emerged on his face. That moment, that look, is forever etched in my memory. I am sure he too would say that moment was unforgettable for him as well."

As Mrs. Bartley spoke her last words, the machines started making sounds no one had heard before. Mr. Bartley's fingers twitched, and his eyelids fluttered.

Valery made a mad dash to the nurses' station. "He's awake, my father is awake!" She needn't have bothered because the nurses had already seen the changes from their monitor and paged all the relevant staff. Doctors and nurses were already on their way to the room.

The doctors asked the family to leave, and they all happily complied. Once in the waiting room, everyone was on their phones calling friends and family.

Mrs. Bartley called her sister in Jamaica. "Monica, do you see how God is good? Just when the doctors wanted us to pull the plug, because they thought there was no hope, God is still steering the ship. Hallelujah."

Valery had just ended a call to her roommate in Atlanta when she saw a robin perched outside the window looking in. She rushed to the window but by the time she got close, the bird flew away. She placed her palm flat against the glass and whispered to herself. "Thanks for everything, Auntie Genie."

Although no longer comatose, Mr. Bartley had more healing to do—he was paralyzed from the hips down. He remained in the hospital for another three weeks under careful observation. Finally, the day came for him to go home.

The hospital staff was sad to see him go because he was such a warm and pleasant patient, but they were happy he was finally able to go home to be with his loved ones. Dr. Malcolm wanted to see the family before they headed out, so he made a quick stop during his rounds.

He stood by Mr. Bartley's bed and held his hand. "After seeing how you have made such a remarkable recovery, I have no doubt in the possibility of you walking again." He shook Mrs. Bartley's hand. "I wish you both all the best. Take care of yourselves." Then he turned to Valery. "Take care of yourself. Okay?"

Valery shook his hand and replied, "I will. We really want to say thanks to you and your team for everything you did for my dad. God bless you all.'"

So excited that her dad was coming home, she wanted to grab the handle of the wheelchair from the hospital orderly who was responsible for bringing her father downstairs and releasing him into their charge. She wanted to wheel him fast down the hall, leaving far behind the room in which he had laid motionless for so long. As a symbolic gesture, she and her mother had agreed they would not turn around to look at the room once their backs were turned.

As they reached the hospital's entrance, they found Jessica waiting with the car. From inside the hospital, a young man called to them. It was Lambert.

He was almost out of breath by the time he reached them. He nodded to Mr. and Mrs. Bartley, but quickly turned to Valery. "I went upstairs, and they told me you guys just left so I caught the elevator and ran as fast as I could to catch up. When are you heading back to Georgia? Or should I ask if you are going back?"

"What is this guy playing at, asking me all these personal questions that have nothing to do with him?" she thought. She was quite anxious to get her dad home to see the rest of the family who were equally anxious for his arrival, but she would not be unkind.

"I am not sure what my next move will be. Why do you ask?"

"I was hoping we could get together before you leave."

She nodded impatiently. "Okay. I will call you as soon as I get myself organized. I still have your card."

Lambert waved at the joyous family as he walked back to the building. Jessica held the back door of the car open as orderlies lifted Mr. Bartley out of the wheelchair and secured him on the back seat of the car. A new wheelchair awaited them at home and other family members would assist them in getting him into bed.

SIX

A week and a half later, Lambert accepted an invitation to Valery's house for "conversation." They sat on the porch—Valery catching up online with friends and family on her laptop, Lambert sitting across from her, enjoying a glass of fresh carrot juice Mrs. Bartley had made.

He attempted to explain to Valery why he had not gone to college as planned. "So," he said, "after my dad got laid off from his job, my mom could not continue to pay the bills by herself, so I got a job in housekeeping at the hospital. Shortly after that, an opportunity for x-ray training came up and I took full advantage of it. So here I am."

Valery stopped what she was doing on the computer and looked at him dead in the face. "So that's it? You don't intend to go to college and law school?"

Lambert sipped his carrot juice. "That's what I want to talk to you about."

"I know you just told me that your family's financial obligations caused you to put a stop to your career goals," said Valery, "but is that really the end for you? Do you still intend to go to college or are you planning on going to college?"

Lambert hesitated and then nodded. "Yes, I intend to go but I do not have the funds right now."

"When will you have the funds?"

"I don't know. Things are hard and I can't save anything right now."

Valery sighed. "Let me get this clear. You are not going to college now because you do not have the money. You want to go but you do not know when you will have the money. Is that what you are telling me?"

Lambert looked at her, a quizzical expression on his face. "Yes, that is exactly what I am telling you. I know you are always so strong and confident, and ever since we were in school, things have always worked out for you. What do I have to do to be like you?"

"Do you know how much money you will need to start?"

"No."

"So, you don't know because when your father lost his job, you cancelled all plans to go to college and you've never bothered to find out. Now you are waiting until you have the money. But you do not know how much money you need and don't know when you will have it."

Lambert set down his glass and leaned back in his chair. *Where is she going with this? Why did I waste my time coming here?*

Valery shook her head. "Let me tell you this, my dear friend. If you truly intend to do anything—and I mean anything—you start with what you have. Since you have no money, start by applying to colleges and asking about scholarships. What types of grants they offer, if any, and how can you qualify? Do something, anything other than just waiting for something to happen. With every action, there is a reaction. But you're not taking action. You must make the first move."

Valery closed her laptop and leaned in toward her friend. She put her hands on his shoulders and gazed in his eyes to make sure he really understood what she was saying to him. "Look at me," she said.

Lambert gladly looked Valery straight in the eyes. What beautiful eyes they are, he thought. As she came closer, his gaze shifted in an awkward, uncomfortable way. He liked being close to Valery, but not this close—especially when her mama was within viewing distance.

She continued. "No, no, no, look at me and listen to what I have to say quite closely. If you don't get it, ask me to repeat it, because I want you to understand."

He leaned back. *Why is she speaking to me like that? Does she think I am slow?*

Pausing just enough to take a quick breath, Valery continued to needle Lambert. "You must have a desire to receive an idea. Your desire is an order to the divine. Your action is the confirmation of your order. Trust me, you will continue to get ideas until you get your desire. As they say, ask and it shall be given."

The sound of a throat being cleared was heard. Mrs. Bartley stood behind them on the porch. "Sorry. Lambert, are you staying for dinner?"

He felt blood rush to his cheeks. "Hmmm, ahhh...I..."

Valery cut him off. "Yes, Mom, he is staying. Thanks for asking."

After dinner, Lambert left the Bartley home feeling empowered. He would act on his desires as Valery had counseled. His first order of business was to get in touch with as many colleges as possible. He made sure to ask the right questions regarding different types of scholarships and their requirements. He asked questions about financial aid and how to qualify. He was on a roll—he would not be passive any longer but instead took an aggressive stance on his future.

Not very long after, and as a show of appreciation, Lambert invited Valery out for dinner. Even though Valery was in her second year of college, she still had to abide by the rules of her parents' house. Out of respect, she asked her mother if she could go.

"If Lambert wants to take you out for dinner," said Mrs. Bartley, "he will have to come to the house and ask."

Despite his newfound confidence, going to a girl's parents to ask permission to take their daughter out for dinner was intimidating for Lambert. But he wanted to show Valery that he respected her and her parents and got their consent the old-fashioned way.

Valery was quite excited for the opportunity to do something that she had not done in a long time. Being away from her friends and college life had made her realize how much she missed socializing with her peers. Dinner with Lambert would be a refreshing change from all that had happened those past few months with her dad.

Lambert was soon to find out that picking up Valery for a simple dinner was not going to be one, two, three. She was also the type of person who did not waste time. While she was waiting on Lambert, she helped her father out of his chair, who was now able to stand, but not without added support. Even so, it was a huge achievement.

"Okay, Dad," she said. "Hold on to me and try to keep your balance. Try to take one step at a time." While Mr. Bartley was trying to maintain his balance, he reminded Valery that she had a date.

"Daddy, if he comes, he will have to wait. You take precedence over everything." She looked at her father and smiled with love and affection in her eyes. "You are the only man in my life."

Mr. Bartley placed his right hand around Valery's shoulder to keep his balance. He smiled softly on the inside at his daughter's comment. "So, what is going on with you guys," he said. "You are about to go on a date with him?"

"Daddy, I am only seventeen with my life ahead of me, and in my second year in college. What could be more important than my ability to secure my means of survival in a way that I can help others? Lambert is a friend and that's all there is to it. I have nothing like that on my radar anytime soon."

Her father looked at her with a knowing look. "Okay, just asking. After all, I am your father and I only have your best interest at heart."

"Enough of that, Daddy. Just see if you can take one step."

Mrs. Bartley walked into the room on her way from watering the plants in the garden.

"Lambert just pulled up and I told him I was coming to get you."

"Okay, Mommy. Tell him I will be right there." She turned back to her father. "Come on, Dad, you can do it."

"I think you should leave this for tomorrow," said her father. "Don't keep Lambert waiting too long."

"Dad, it's up to you. I'm not leaving until you take a step."

Knowing how stubborn his daughter was, Mr. Bartley gave it all he got. He pursed his lips, held a firm grip around Valery's waist, and groaned. He tried to make his feet do what he had been trying to make them do for many days, but nothing happened.

"Come on, Dad. Do not think about your feet. Think of walking. That is what you have done all your life. Do you remember you used to run behind my bike when you were teaching me to ride? You said, 'Don't think about the wheels, think about riding.'"

Mr. Bartley's thoughts took him to that moment as if it were happening again. He remembered the moment when Valery first managed to balance the bike as it rolled down the driveway toward the street and Valery could not stop it, and how frightened he was as he ran and grabbed the bike. The memory of that moment was so real and vivid that Mr. Bartley did not realize he had moved his left leg.

He came back to the present at the sound of Valery's loud voice. "Dad, you did it! Oh, my word, oh, wow!"

Mrs. Bartley heard the uproar and rushed back inside the room to find out what had happened. She arrived in bare feet—not realizing that she'd left her slippers somewhere between the garden and the bedroom upstairs. Bursting through the door and out of breath, she saw her husband and daughter sharing a joyful moment, and her fright turned into relief. "What happened?"

"He just made a step," said Valery. "Daddy made a step."

"What? Are you kidding?" Mrs. Bartley looked up to the ceiling, raising her hands to God. "Thank you, thank you, God, for blessing my husband's feet, amen." She opened her arms to encircle them in a group hug.

Lambert's patience was wearing down a bit. He was on time and now he had to wait, and he was starving. As he was getting out of his car to find out what was taking so long, he heard sounds of laughter coming from the house. As soon as he opened the gate, he saw Valery emerge from the doorway and walked down the steps towards him. A big smile was on her face.

"What's going on?" he said. "You look like you just won some big money." He held the gate open for her.

"Much more than that my dear good friend. Much more than that."

She walked to the passenger side of the car and waited for Lambert to open the door. Seeing that he was about to get in the car on the driver's side, she cleared her throat. He was a little annoyed but remembered that Valery was raised with old-fashioned values. Her dad had taught her what she should expect from a man when he took her out.

As Lambert opened the car door, she looked at him, her eyes twinkling. "My dad just made his first step to recovery."

Once inside the car, Lambert looked at Valery with genuine interest. "It is really great that your dad took a step but exactly what happened?" Valery had that infectious smile that makes you want to smile too, and Lambert did.

"Can you imagine? My father just moved one of his legs and made a step. The same man they said would never walk again."

Lambert was in total disbelief. "What? Do you mean your father actually got out of the wheelchair and stood up? Wow! That *is* amazing."

He started the car and drove off. "It's amazing what our minds can do for us if we really try," said Valery. "The more I see, the more I come to know that all things are really possible to him that believes."

Lambert smiled. "Amen to that my dear sister. It is quite so. Trust me."

Distracted by their conversation, Lambert almost drove through a red light. "Watch it," Valery shouted. He stepped on the brake quickly, then backed up behind the red light and waited. A police car was coming from the opposite direction. When the light changed, a female voice on the loudspeaker of the police car said, "Be careful, and keep your eyes on the road." Lambert blushed.

The young couple arrived safely at the restaurant and were ready to enjoy a pleasant meal together. During the course of the meal, Lambert had the bright idea to order wine. He summoned the waiter over to place the order. When Valery heard what Lambert ordered she quickly shut it down.

She looked at Lambert quite sternly. "Wine! What are we doing with wine? I am only seventeen and in case you do not know, I am not allowed to drink. Plus, you are not supposed to drink and drive either. What are we doing here?"

Lambert shrugged. "I just wanted the moment to be special."

"Special? What is so special about having dinner? You are my friend and you asked me out for dinner."

Lambert cut in before Valery could finish what she was about to say. "Alright, alright. Sorry. Maybe I went too far, but I brought you here to say thanks so, so much…and to let you know that I got accepted into college."

Valery shook her head and her eyes brightened. "What? Congratulations! When did this happen?"

"Last week. And…I received a full scholarship as well."

"Amazing."

Lambert reached his hands across the table taking Valery's hands. She put down her knife and fork and held his hands in hers. "I am so sorry for my behavior. I had no idea."

He smiled. "Thanks so much for your words of encouragement. I thought about everything you said that evening. I cannot thank you enough because you have no idea the impact your words had on my ability to take charge of the direction I want my life to go. You dished it out without apology. Your rebuke did not feel wrong and that is the mark of a true friend because I realized your words were delivered with sincerity of heart."

Valery blushed. "We are all here to brace each other up, whatever it takes. I am sure you would do the same for me." She picked up her utensils, "Now, let us finish this lovely meal and no wine, okay?"

Lambert laughed. "Okay, okay. No wine it is."

The rest of the evening was light-hearted, full of reminiscing from their school days—a memorable night for both of them.

SEVEN

After her father's return home, Valery's mom relied upon her a great deal to assist with her father's care and emotional wellbeing, so she decided not to return to college right away. Being a part of the accelerated program in high school had allowed her to move ahead and start college two years ahead of her peers and this allowed her to take time off to be home with her parents.

She wanted to wait until her father fully recovered anyway—she knew that she probably would not be at her best in school as she would worry about how her father was getting along and the toll of being a caregiver would have on her mom, so she took a job at her previous high school as an assistant counselor.

One evening, while Valery was leaving work, she had a strong taste for mangoes, so she decided to make a quick stop at the fruit and vegetable market to see if there were any. Lucky for her there was a great variety to choose from. She made her purchase and headed out the door for home.

Up ahead, she saw an old woman pushing a shopping cart across the street. The woman had not crossed in the proper place and was having difficulty getting her cart up on the curb. No one had stopped to help. Valery watched as she pulled on the handle several times trying to get her cart to go over the curb, but her weak, frail arms could not manage it. On her last attempt, the cart toppled over and some of her groceries spilled out.

Valery hurried across the street just in time to rescue an onion that was heading into traffic. "Are you okay?" she said, holding out the onion.

The old woman smiled. "Thank you, my dear."

Valery righted the cart and got busy picking up the rest of the spilled groceries. When she was done, she pulled the cart up onto the curb and instructed the woman to cross at the pedestrian crossing where the sidewalk was level with the street.

"God bless you, my child," said the woman with gratitude. "What is your name?"

"I am Valery. And what is yours?"

"My name is Rebecca Canon. But everyone calls me Auntie Becca, whether they are family or not."

"So, Auntie Becca, how far do you have to go?"

The woman pointed in the direction of the Methodist Church. "Not too far—just up there on Finch Avenue. It is the second house on the right."

From where they stood, Finch Avenue was two long blocks away and the thought of this frail woman pulling her cart that far did not sit well with Valery's conscience. She looked at her watch and realized she had enough time to continue her good deed. "You know what, Auntie Becca? I am going to walk with you. Is that okay?"

The woman's face lit up. "Thank you so much. Normally the cart wouldn't be so heavy, but I could not help myself when I saw all those sale items. I bought too many things."

"That's okay. Today is your lucky day." Valery said as she pushed the cart with her pocketbook tucked under her arm.

"I know you are young and strong but let me help you too," said the woman.

"It's okay Auntie, I can manage."

"No, let me carry your pocketbook."

"Oh, okay, if you insist. Thank you so much."

Auntie Becca took the pocketbook from under Valery's arm. "You see one hand washes the other, right?" They both laughed as they walked up the street to Finch Avenue.

Valery could tell from the houses and the well-manicured lawns that the neighborhood they were entering was rather ritzy. When they finally arrived at Finch, Auntie Becca said, "Turn left here." As they approached the second house on the right. Valery's eyes grew large. *This house is like all the others we have passed. It is so very big, and look at the garden, what magnificent flowers. I could roll around on that lush grass all day, if I was ten years old again, that is.*

As they walked up the driveway, a car rolled in behind them and Valery pulled the cart out of the way to allow it to pass and park inside the garage.

"That's my son," said Auntie Becca. "He is so protective of me."

"He would not be a good son if he was not protective of his mother," Valery said with a smile on her face.

"Well, these days, it's hard to find someone as kind and honest as you. Anybody else might have run away with my cart."

"True," said Valery. "And just any elderly person might have run away with my pocketbook."

Both laughed. "Can you imagine an old lady like me running away with your pocketbook?"

"You never know," said Valery. "You could be a retired track star."

Auntie Becca waited for her son to exit his car. As he walked over to the two of them, he reached into his pocket. "Thank you for helping my mother. How much do I owe you?"

"Nothing," said Valery.

He jerked the cart from her. "How much do you want?"

Before Valery could respond, Auntie Becca raised her voice to her son. "No need to be so rude. I can pay this young woman if I want to. After all, she was just being kind and helpful."

"Who is she anyway?"

The old woman's voice grew louder. "I warn you, watch your tongue. I was having a bit of difficulty with the shopping cart, and she helped me. Plus, the cart was heavy, and she wanted to make sure that I got home safely. Is that so terrible?"

The man's face was now red. "Mom," he said, "I told you to let me know when you want to go shopping."

"I needed some exercise and a change of scenery, so I decided to walk to the supermarket myself to pick up a few items."

"Why didn't you ask the housekeeper to go with you? Where is she?"

"I suppose she is somewhere inside. I do not need to have people following me around, catering to my every move. Please take the cart inside while I see my friend off."

Valery was stunned to hear the woman speak with such authority to her grown son. They watched as he walked away pushing the shopping cart and then the old woman turned to Valery. "Can you stay for dinner?"

"Thanks for the invitation, ma'am…I mean Auntie… but I must hurry back to my car. I wasn't parked in such a great spot. I hope I am spared a ticket." She turned and started for the sidewalk. "It was a pleasure meeting you," she said.

When she got to the end of the driveway, the old woman called after her. "Valery, you left your pocketbook."

When Valery rushed back to retrieve the purse, the old woman stopped her. "We can't stay in touch without exchanging phone numbers." She pulled out a card from her purse and handed it to Valery. It was a simple card, with only the woman's full name, phone number and home address. Valery quickly scribbled her name and information on paper she found in her pocketbook and gave it to the woman.

"Thank you, my dear," said the woman. "I will be checking up on you." *That's a very special girl,* the woman thought to herself as she watched her new friend disappear around the corner. She smiled and turned to enter the house through the open garage door.

EIGHT

The following evening when Valery got home from work, she was surprised to find her parents waiting in the living room for her. The look of concern on their faces was not a good sign. Her mother was holding a letter in her hand. *What could it be? Was it news from Jamaica that a relative had died?*

"Good evening, guys," she said. "Is everything okay? You don't look so good."

Mrs. Bartley looked at her husband and back at Valery.

"What is going on? Why the silence? Can somebody say something?"

Mrs. Bartley's gaze went down to the floor. She extended her hand with the letter toward Valery, who took it and read. The letter was from the bank informing them that their house was in foreclosure.

Valery stared at her parents in disbelief. "You mean we were behind on the mortgage, and nobody bothered to say anything to me? I may be seventeen years old, but I am still a part of this family and I live here."

Finally, Mrs. Bartley broke the silence. "As you are well aware your father was unable to work since he had the accident, and his case is still in court."

"We did not want to burden you with our problem," said Mr. Bartley. "My brother promised to help me out until the case was settled but I have not been able to catch up with him. Things will work out, I promise."

Valery shook her head. "Dad, you know your brother. He did not even come to visit you when you were at your worst. Do you think you can depend on him now? It is evident he is in no rush to come to your rescue."

She sat on the couch beside her mother. "You know what? We are not going to lose our house. I am going to make sure of that."

"Valery, what are you talking about? We will not allow you to take on our burden."

"No, Mother, this is now *our* burden."

"How are you going to save this house?"

"Don't you worry about how."

"I know you mean well, dear, but it is too late—there is nothing to be done."

Valery's phone rang. She did not realize she was still holding it when she came through the door. She looked at it and saw that it was her new friend Auntie Becca. She was not in the mood to talk to her, so she turned off the ringer and let the call go to voicemail.

Valery was determined to save her parents' house, so the following day she started her mission to find a second job. She went to restaurants, supermarkets, department stores, office buildings—and applied for any type of work that was available, anything she could do in the evenings or on weekends.

For several days, Valery pounded the pavement sometimes with small hopes of hearing, "If we are interested, we will contact you." Eventually, though, the strain of finding a second job, the possibility of losing the home she lived in, and feeling tired all the time put her out of sorts with herself. It was not until she reached home at night that she even looked at her phone and would see she had missed calls. Auntie Becca had called her multiple times and she was upset with herself for not being more vigilant. By the time she saw that the old woman had called, it was always too late to call her back.

Valery was on lunch break at the school where she worked when her telephone rang. It was Auntie Becca.

"Have you been avoiding me? I called you so many times. Were you travelling?"

"No, I have been so busy I hardly have time for myself."

"Oh, you are working *and* going to school?"

"No, I am not going to school right now and after work I have so many things to do. Sometimes I get home very late."

The school bell rang, and Auntie Becca asked her, "What's that sound?"

"Oh, it's the school bell. I'm not *in* school, but I work there, and I have to go now. I promise I will call you as soon as I get the chance to talk longer."

Valery's persistence finally landed her two extra jobs—cleaning offices in the evenings after her job at the school and babysitting for a nice couple not too far from her home on the weekends.

She contacted the bank on behalf of her parents but

could not come up with an agreement that would satisfy them. She was determined to help her parents keep their house so she contacted a lawyer for help. He said he would try his best and that was enough to keep her hoping.

Two weeks went by, and Valery paid a visit to the attorney's office. Unfortunately, he did not have encouraging news. He informed her that it was already too late to turn things around without a lot of cash and that they should prepare to start packing. "I am so sorry. Maybe if you had come to me sooner there might have been some hope, but as it stands the process has gone too far now. The brokerage firm who holds the mortgage is about to set a date for auction."

On her way home, Valery wondered how to tell her parents that the house inevitably would go up for auction if they could not raise some money soon. Where would they go? Her uncle who'd promised to help them had not called as he said he would. Tears streamed down her cheeks.

Valery stopped her car on a quiet street near a park. She switched off the ignition and took deep cleansing breaths as she tried to dry her tears. She closed her eyes to concentrate on her breath when her telephone rang. It was Auntie Becca again, whom she had promised to call now over a month earlier. Although she was fond of the old woman, she did not want to talk to anyone.

As she sat in her car, pondering the fate of her family and their home, a sense of urgency crept up from the pit of her stomach. "What am I missing?" She thought again. "I need to just relax and calm myself," she said aloud.

Valery leaned back in the seat, closed her eyes, and inhaled deeply. After a few minutes, in her mind's eye, a robin lit on the steering wheel and she awakened to a new revelation. She had forgotten the fundamental truth she had shared with people repeatedly—the power of the imagination.

As quickly as her anxiety had come, it went. The weight fell from her shoulders, and she laughed. "Oh, my goodness! To think I have all this time been worrying myself needlessly. How did I manage to sink so deeply in the external world where everything is already happening?"

She continued talking to herself. "The woman in my dream told me how one can change the present."

With that thought, she paused, her eyebrows pinched together, and her forehead wrinkled with memories of her conversation with the woman in her dream. Her face brightened up and her red eyes opened wide as though waiting for the world to be swallowed up in them.

Suddenly, she was filled with joy and the understanding that everything in the present moment was created in the past. She looked around to see if anyone noticed her excitement before she continued quietly talking to herself. "So, the present moment is the future of the past and if I spend the present moment worrying about the past, my future will be the same as my past and that is where imagination comes in. To imagine something different from the present is the creation of a different future." She stopped and breathed again.

"From this moment on, I will not worry. I will start to imagine my family and me living in our house instead of worrying about losing it and where we would go." Valery freshened up her face and drove toward home.

When she got there, she met her father's physical therapist as he was leaving the house and opened the gate to let him through.

"Hello Mr. Uzu, how are you?"

After exchanging pleasantries, the therapist updated her about Mr. Bartley's progress. "Your father is doing well."

Mrs. Bartley was standing outside the door at the top of the steps waiting for her daughter. When Valery reached the top of the steps, she wrapped her arms around her mom and planted a big kiss on her cheek. "Good evening, Mom. How is my favorite mother?"

"Your favorite mother? I thought I was the only one." They both laughed as they continued to embrace each other.

"You are really happy—glowing this evening. Are you in love? Did you hear from Lambert?"

Valery released the embrace. "No, Mom," she said. Let's go inside."

Mr. Bartley was in the living room watching television.

"Hi, Dad," said Valery. "I hear you are doing very well."

Mr. Bartley had not been using his wheelchair for some weeks. He was deftly mastering the use of his walker. He pushed it away to make space for his daughter. "Come and sit beside me and tell me why you are looking so happy. Have you met someone?"

"Does the source of one's happiness always have to be from a man?"

While the two were busy chatting away, Mrs. Bartley was preparing dinner. At the table, Valery asked if she could do the honor of saying the grace. At the end of her prayer, she said, "And thank you for this lovely house that holds so many memories for this family."

Her parents looked quizzically at each other, then at Valery, but they all said "Amen" in unison.

"Valery, dear, is there something you are not telling us?"

"Why would you say that, Daddy?"

"There is something strange about your behavior," said her mother. "First you were worried about losing our house and now you are thanking God for it."

"Come now, Mother, there is nothing fishy going on, I can assure you."

Mr. Bartley cleared his throat. "Did you hear from the lawyer? What did he say? If you know something, please tell us. There is an aura of peace and tranquility glowing on your face. Please share the source of this joy so we can understand."

Valery did not entertain their eagerness to get inside her head. She ignored their questions and focused on the meal set before her. She cut her dumpling into bite-sized pieces. She scooped some beans onto her fork and popped the delectable beans into her mouth. "Mmmmm, that's delicious. Finally, she set down her fork and turned to her parents.

"Okay, Mom and Dad. The reason for my renewed self is that I have decided I will no longer worry myself about things that I cannot change, and I will not let anything from the past prevent me from making the best of my present moment. Will it change anything if we worry and make ourselves sick? Life goes on regardless of our present situation. The important question to ask is what is to be done with what remains before us."

Mr. Bartley was pleased to hear his little girl speak with so much conviction. "You've never failed to make me so proud of you."

Mrs. Bartley sipped some of her soursop juice. "I agree with your dad. Whenever you make a commitment, you always follow through. That is a good quality you have. At least now we know why you are so upbeat today."

NINE

Valery's dad heard the sound of something being placed in the letterbox outside and looked up from the newspaper he was reading. He had not spoken to John, the mailman, in quite some time and wanted to say hello.

Mr. Bartley opened the door just in time to catch John before he disappeared down the sidewalk. "Thank you, John for the delivery. How are you doing? It is so good to see you."

The mailman turned around and gasped. Holding carefully to the rails, Mr. Bartley was making his way down the steps toward him. He had heard about Mr. Bartley's accident and the possibility of him not walking again, but had not seen him since that horrible day.

"Mr. Bartley, I cannot believe my eyes," he said as he turned back to greet him. John gave him a hearty handshake, while looking at him from head to toe. "Sir, I am so happy for you. This is nothing short of a lovely miracle."

Mr. Bartley smiled and said, "The doctors claimed I would never walk again but doctors are not God. X-rays and scans can see but so much into the human body. You can see the physical heart, but you cannot see how much love is in it. You can see the brain, but you cannot see the mind."

John adjusted the mailbag on his shoulder. "Wow those are some profound words of wisdom, sir. You really made my day today. You gave me something to think about."

"I owe it to my daughter. I don't know what I would do without her."

"You have a special child there."

"I am forever grateful to have her."

The two men shook hands again and parted company. Mr. Bartley watched as John walked to deliver the mail to his next-door neighbor and hobbled back up the steps to fetch the mail from the letterbox.

Once inside, he made himself comfortable on the sofa. He laid the mail on the coffee table and sorted through it to see which envelopes looked important and finally settled on one. After he read the letter, he calmly got up and walked to the kitchen. He fetched himself a glass from the cabinet and poured water from the fridge. After drinking half a glass, he walked to the kitchen window with the rest. He stood there gazing at nothing in particular.

He did not hear when his wife returned home. Usually she made a racket, especially when she went grocery shopping. She walked into the kitchen only to find him still there. "Linton, is everything okay?"

He set the glass of water on the table. "I am so sorry, dear. I am afraid I am not myself right now." He shrugged and handed her the letter. "This just came today. We have only two months to leave."

She grabbed the letter and read what she had feared was coming but still could not wrap her head around it.

Her legs felt like Jello under her weight, so she quickly pulled out a chair from the table. She read the letter again and let it sink in. Tears flowed down her cheeks. "Why is this happening? I mean, I know why it is happening, but where are we going to go?"

Her husband bent over and hugged her. "Don't worry, honey. No matter what the outcome, we will be just fine."

Mrs. Bartley pulled herself away from her husband and stood there looking at him. "Fine? Just fine? Linton! We are losing our house and you are talking about things will be just fine. How, may I ask?"

She flung the letter down on the table and walked into the living room, threw herself on the couch, and cried even more. Mr. Bartley sat down beside his wife. "If I had not had the accident, nothing like this would have happened."

She quickly sat up and curled her arms around his neck. She spoke softly. "It's not your fault. It's not your fault at all. You are my life and I love you. Do not blame yourself. It is just so hard to see everything we have worked for taken away just like that."

Mr. Bartley dried her tears. "I have never doubted your love for me and no matter how things turn out you will always be the love of my life. By the help of God, we will be okay."

She sighed. "But what are we going to do? Where will we go? It will be so embarrassing for our child."

"My dear Yvette, there is nothing we can do right now. We must accept the fact that we will have to leave this house. We offered to catch up on the back payments and they refused anything we had to offer."

"That is because they want to take our house and sell it at a much higher price. How could they be so wicked?"

Mr. Bartley got up to get water from the kitchen for his wife. He noticed the bags she brought back from shopping, so he decided to unpack them for her since she was not in a frame of mind to do anything.

He looked in the largest bag first and saw a cake box. He picked up the box, opened it, and saw that it was a cake for Valery's birthday. He shook his head, embarrassed that he had missed the fact. He closed the box, placed it back in the bag, and took up the glass.

He returned to the living room and handed his wife the water. "How selfish of me. Our daughter is eighteen today, and I did not even remember. Can you imagine?"

Mrs. Bartley sipped a little of the water. "Valery is working so hard that I don't think the poor thing realized herself that today is her birthday, so I decided to surprise her with a cake." A sob escaped from her lips.

"Honey, it is breaking my heart to see you cry like this," he said. He went down on both knees and rested his head in her lap. "It feels like every drop of your tears is draining the blood from my heart. I would do anything to see you smile again. Let them take the house as long as that loss does not break us apart."

Hearing those words from her husband's lips and knowing that they were coming from his heart made her realize that she was brought to sadness because of her own thinking. Mrs. Bartley had fooled herself into believing that it would be a disgrace if they lost their house. She was worried about what people would say. Of all the things in the world, she had something that most women lived, hoped, and died wanting. Something more precious than money, a car, a house or fine jewelry, and that was the true, undying, everlasting love of a good man.

She was so overwhelmed that she cupped her husband's face in her hands. She kissed the lids of his eyes, the tip of his nose, his cheeks and finally his lips.

The passion rose up in them. Without saying a word, they retreated to the bedroom and expressed their undying love, each surrendering to one another. The two spirits became one and once again created a magic that brought joy to their hearts.

In a while, husband and wife left the bedroom renewed in mind and body. No challenge the world brought was going to sow division in their hearts. They made up in their minds that happiness was more important. They both agreed they would not tell Valery the news until after her birthday was over.

With that, Mrs. Bartley called Jessica and Lambert and all the neighbors and friends she could think of and threw herself into decorating the living room with the help of her husband. They were like little kids blowing balloons and tossing them at each other. When they were done, the table was covered with all of Valery's favorite finger foods and snacks. It was beautiful. Valery was sure to be surprised.

A few hours later, Mrs. Barkley heard voices outside and peeped through the curtain by the window. Lambert was at the door and Valery was berating him about being there without having notified her first. Everyone else was in place and quiet. The stage was set.

Valery opened the door and glanced around. "Maybe they went out and did not get back yet. But why didn't they leave the light on?"

"You know these old folks don't think sometimes," said Lambert.

Valery was annoyed. "Please do not refer to my parents as old folks. They are Mr. Linton and Mrs. Yvette Bartley to you, and I'll thank you to remember that." Everyone in the room held their breath so as not to burst into laughter.

"Now where is that switch…" said Valery. When she found it and flipped it on, the room erupted into shouts of "Surprise!" Valery was so startled she dropped her handbag and keys and grabbed onto Lambert. The Bartleys grinned. Their surprise party was truly a surprise!

Valery buried her face in Lambert's chest for a brief moment, no doubt to hide her embarrassment, and apologized for yelling at him. She turned to face everyone and to take in the beautiful decorations and all the smiling faces of friends and relatives who had come at last minute to celebrate her special day. She was overjoyed, smiling from ear to ear.

After the celebration was over, Valery's closest and favorite cousin Jessica was the last to leave. Valery walked her to the gate to see her off.

"That was really sweet of your parents to throw you this birthday surprise," said Jessica.

"Yes, indeed. It was a lovely distraction. I love chocolate cake and ice cream."

They embraced and parted company and Valery watched until Jessica drove away. Still on a sugar high, she climbed the steps two at a time. She was determined to celebrate with as much cake as possible. Nothing was going to diminish her joy.

Once inside the house, it looked like her parents were having just as much fun pulling down the decorations as they had had putting them up.

"Wow, you guys got me really good," said Valery. "My birthday was the last thing on my mind. Thank you so much."

Mr. Bartley picked up a trash bag but before he walked out the door, he smiled at his daughter. "Aww, how could I forget your birthday? You have inspired us so much."

"Dad, are you sure you can carry that bag?"

"The way I feel right now, I could carry this bag and *you.*" He gave a big belly laugh.

"I wish my birthday could come more often. It's a long time since I have seen this kind of happiness from you guys. It is good to see your smiling faces again."

Valery's cell phone rang and her mother, near the coffee table where the phone lay, brought it to her. Seeing who it was, Valery quickly answered it. "Hello, Auntie Becca, how are you doing?"

"My dear girl, have you forgotten about me? I have

been trying to catch up with you for the longest time. Have you decided to abandon this poor little old lady?"

"Oh, no, Auntie Becca, I have not. Please do not say that." Valery's parents looked at each other quizzically. Auntie Becca?

Seeing the inquiring look on their faces, she went to her room for privacy. "Yes, Auntie," she explained to the old woman, "I just came upstairs to my room away from the prying ears of my parents. I came home a little earlier today and was planning to call you, but I came home to a surprise birthday party. I'm eighteen years old today."

"Well, congratulations to you," said the old woman. "I certainly hope you are having a lovely evening."

Valery heard grandmotherly warmth in her voice, which made her smile. She plunked herself down on the bed. "Oh, yes, I had a really nice time. I had no idea."

The woman cleared her throat. "Then I would love to take you out to dinner tomorrow. We will celebrate your birthday again. I will not accept no for an answer."

Valery thought for a moment. She would have to skip her cleaning job but…"Okay, it's a promise. I am definitely looking forward to spending some time with you. Dinner is hard to resist."

The old woman gave Valery the address where to meet her, a fancy restaurant downtown. "Don't be late," she said, "and come very hungry." They both laughed as they hung up.

Valery lolled about in her room for about an hour and then wandered downstairs to see if there was anything left for her to help with, but she was too late. Her parents had everything under control. The place looked as it was before the party—spic and span. Her dad had settled himself down in front of the television. Mrs. Bartley waited at the bottom of the stairs with cake on a fork. "Open up." Mrs. Bartley stuck the sweet morsel in Valery's mouth. Mr. Bartley saw the playful exchange and laughed.

"Don't just stand there. Come over here. We need to hear about this Auntie Becca."

Valery giggled. "Mom, were you on your way to my room to bribe me with more cake?"

"Yes. Now you are going to tell us about this mysterious caller of yours." Mrs. Bartley ushered her daughter into the living room and plopped her down beside her father before taking a seat herself on Valery's other side. "Now that you have eaten my bribe tell us about this aunt we have never met."

Smiling, Valery looked at both parents sitting on either side of her. She reached for the remote and turned off the television.

"Ok, here we go. I was leaving the supermarket a couple of months ago when I saw an elderly woman crossing the street with her shopping cart. But when she got to the other side, she could not get the cart onto the sidewalk. It slipped out of her hands and some of her groceries fell out. I helped her to pick up her stuff and I pushed it two blocks to her home for her and we became friends. We exchanged numbers. We call each other from time to time. Her name is Rebecca, but she said I could call her Auntie Becca."

Mrs. Bartley said, "Is she Jamaican?"

Valery shook her head. "I don't know. I did not detect an accent." She paused. "She wants to take me to dinner for my birthday tomorrow after work."

Mr. Barkley frowned. "Shouldn't someone accompany you?"

Valery shook her head and laughed. "Dad, I just turned eighteen. I do not need someone to protect me from a little old lady." She hugged both her parents and thanked them again for the surprise.

TEN

Valery was successful at finding someone to cover for her at her cleaning job. She left early from work at the school. The dinner reservation was set for five, which gave her enough time to rush home to freshen up and choose something nice to wear.

The old woman was at the restaurant by four-thirty to make sure that the cake she'd ordered was delivered on time and that it was beautifully decorated. She told the restaurant manager that she would let them know when to bring out the cake, so everyone knew it was a surprise. While she waited, she saw a lawyer who had worked for her late husband's company, which now belonged to her and her son. "Mr. Brown," she called. The man turned in the direction of the voice and walked over to her.

"Mrs. Canon, how are you?"

"I am quite fine. I'm waiting for my daughter, who should be here any minute now. How is my son treating you?"

"I cannot complain," he said, but looked confused. "I had no idea you had a daughter."

"There is a lot you don't know about me, Mr. Brown."

Valery was happy to see the old woman waiting for her. She walked up behind her and planted a kiss on her cheek. "Hi, Auntie Becca," she said.

The woman quickly turned around. "Hello, my dear. You gave me such a fright!"

"I am so sorry. I was so happy to see you."

"Let me introduce you to a friend of the family," said Auntie Becca.

Valery looked up into the face of the lawyer she had visited to help save her parents' house.

The man looked as though he had seen a ghost. His face went from flushed to pale in an instant.

"Mrs. Canon, I am so sorry. I had no idea. Why did your son make that decision?"

Auntie Becca frowned. "What are you talking about?" Valery and Mr. Brown were both obviously uncomfortable, and the wise old lady realized very quickly that they knew each other.

"What is going on here?" She stood up, her eyes burning into Mr. Brown.

"May I talk to you outside?" She turned to Valery. "Please excuse me for a few minutes, dear."

Outside, Mrs. Canon looked at the young lawyer. "Explain to me," she said, "how you know her."

Mr. Brown swallowed hard.

"Well, ma'am, she came to me about her parents' house with a letter about foreclosure. I recognized that the letter was on your company letterhead and immediately called your son. He told me to let her know that things had progressed too far and that nothing was going to reverse the process. She returned two weeks later to follow up and that is when I relayed the message. Until just now, I hadn't seen her again." He paused. "I'm confused. Are you saying your son foreclosed on your daughter?"

"Let's go back inside, shall we?" As they walked back to her table, Mrs. Canon said to the man, "Please join us for dinner and I'll explain. But first, I need you to do something for me…and quickly."

When she returned to the table, Mrs. Canon told Valery she had invited Mr. Brown to join them for dinner. Although still confused and a little bit angry, Valery accepted the news with grace. After a few moments, he approached them and pulled out a chair.

"Let me clear things up for you, Mr. Brown," said the woman. "No, technically, I do not have a daughter. After my son was born, I was advised not to have more children, but this young woman, in spirit, is the daughter I always dreamed of." Valery blushed and Mr. Brown nodded his head in understanding.

Dinner was delicious. They all enjoyed what they selected from the menu. Valery said no each time Mrs. Canon asked if she wanted more to eat. "The food here is out of this world, Auntie Becca," she said, "but I always leave room for dessert."

"Well, then," said Mrs. Canon. "Let's proceed." The old woman signaled to one of the waiters, who brought out a cake and set it down in front of Valery. All the waiters and servers sang "Happy Birthday" as they approached the table.

Valery looked at the cake. The words on the cake read, "To Valery: Happy 18th Birthday." The decorations were like fine art—it was almost a shame to put a knife through it.

Overcome with emotion, Valery covered her face with her hands and wept. When she had finally composed herself, she kissed the old woman on both cheeks, thanking her profusely. She had not expected such a magnificent meal, much less this mouthwatering dessert, from someone she hardly knew.

While the candles on the cake were being lit by one of the restaurant staff, a person appeared beside the table and handed Mrs. Canon a big brown envelope, which she placed in her lap out of sight. With the last candle lit, she said, "Okay, my dear, make your wish and blow out your candles."

Valery closed her eyes and imagined her family smiling and happy and living in their house, something she had been doing every night before she went to sleep. She opened her eyes slowly, took a deep breath, and blew out all the candles.

Mrs. Canon raised her glass to propose a toast to Valery's happy future. "May your future be bright and full of endless possibilities. May you continue to be sweet, caring and unselfish—we need more people like you in the world."

Valery grinned and held up her glass of sparkling apple cider. "Thank you, Auntie Becca. This evening has meant the world to me."

It was getting late, and Mr. Brown stood to thank Mrs. Canon for the wonderful dinner and to wish Valery a happy birthday again.

"Don't leave just yet," said the woman. She pulled the envelope from her lap and placed it on the table. She removed some papers, signed them, and then passed the documents to Valery. "Happy Birthday. These papers are my gift to you. But you must sign them as well."

Puzzled, Valery looked down at the papers. "I don't understand, Auntie Becca. You know I can't sign these without looking at them, even on your say so."

The old woman smiled proudly. "You are a smart girl, Valery, and I did not expect you to. Take your time to read closely what I have handed you."

Bewildered, Valery glanced down and began to read. The young lawyer leaned in. "Do you have any idea what you have in front of you?"

Before Valery could respond, Mrs. Canon said, "It's okay, Mr. Brown, I will explain." She adjusted herself in her seat, displaying grace and poise as she did so, and went straight to the point. "Valery, it is my understanding that your parents have lost their house in foreclosure."

Blood rushed to Valery's cheeks. She looked at the lawyer with anger and embarrassment. He'd disclosed her personal affairs to someone she barely knew. She forced a smile and straightened her shoulders.

"Auntie Becca, I am very grateful for what you have done for me this evening, acknowledging my birthday by inviting me to share a meal with you, not to mention this lovely cake. I appreciate it all, but whatever is in these papers I cannot accept. Please, I must go now." She picked up her pocketbook and stood up to leave.

The old woman stood too and spoke softly but firmly. "Please sit, my dear." Melting at the firm tone of her voice,

Valery looked into Auntie Becca's eyes and felt a shimmer of electricity move down her spine. They all sat back down.

"What I am trying to tell you," said the old woman, "is that I own the company that holds the mortgage on your parents' house."

Valery's eyes became as wide as a dinner plate. "What!?" She looked at the lawyer in disbelief. He leaned back in his chair and waited patiently for Mrs. Canon's next words.

"What you have in front of you are the deed to your house and notification that the mortgage on the home—the one in which you live now—is now paid. The lien is released. You and your parents owe nothing—the house is yours, free and clear."

Valery could not wrap her head around what was happening. She wanted to make sure the words coming out of the woman's mouth were real and that she was not dreaming. "Auntie Becca, can you repeat that?"

Mrs. Canon beamed. "Indeed. The house in which you live is now *yours*—assuming you sign these papers. Mike will be our witness and will record the legal transaction first thing tomorrow." Pulling her chair closer to Valery's, she arranged the papers in front of the young woman and said, "Please, sign right here, and right here, and right here."

After Valery finished signing all the papers, she placed one set back in the envelope and handed it to the lawyer. She held her copies to her chest and cried softly.

ELEVEN

It was all Valery could do not to run all the way home. As soon as she got inside the house, she threw her pocketbook on the sofa and called for her parents, who came from the kitchen. She waved the papers in front of them. "I bet you can't guess what these papers are."

Her father seemed annoyed. "Look, Valery, there is no time for guessing games right now. Your mother and I have a more pressing issue to discuss with you."

"Yes," said her mother. "Let him speak, dear. We have been waiting for you all evening to tell you what has happened."

Mr. Bartley nodded. "We didn't want to disturb you on your birthday, but we received bad news about the house."

Valery interrupted him. "Yes, but Daddy—"

"Wait, let me finish." He held up the letter in his hand. "I know you instructed us to imagine ourselves living in this house. We tried that, and nothing came of it. This letter is telling us we have to vacate immediately."

"I've called my brother Albert," said her mother, "and he and his family will allow us to stay with them until we can find an apartment. Unlike your dad's brother, mine knows we would have done the same for him. It's all right, though. At least we have each other."

Valery burst into uncontrollable laughter. She grabbed the letter from her father and tore it to pieces.

For a moment, her parents thought she had gone mad. They were now even more convinced that the stress of losing their home was too much for the poor child to bear, especially when she held the papers she was holding in the air and declared at the top of her voice, "We are not going anywhere because *I* am the owner of this house."

Mrs. Bartley looked at her husband. "Call emergency." Before her father could reach for his phone, Valery grabbed it from the table. "Sit down, please, and listen to me."

She gave them a full account of her evening with Mrs. Canon and Mr. Brown and then handed them the papers to read. "This is what she gave me for my birthday."

As Valery's parents read the papers, relief spread across their faces. Mrs. Bartley rose to her feet and paced the floor with her hands held high in praise. "Thank you, Heavenly Father," she said. "Thank you."

Her father fought hard to hold back a single tear that fell from his eye. Valery wiped it from his cheek with the back of her hand.

The next morning when Valery awoke, a little robin sat on the ledge outside her window. She heard Auntie Genie's words. "What we imagine is what we are creating for ourselves. Our lives are the results of our thoughts."

TWELVE

The doorbell rang at the Bartley's home. Mrs. Bartley looked through the peephole to see a well-dressed woman standing there. She opened the door.

The woman smiled. "May I come in?" she asked.

"Certainly," said Mrs. Bartley, stepping out of the doorway. "Linton, we have a visitor!" she called. She guided the woman into their living room and offered her something to drink. Mr. Bartley joined them and holding out his hand, looked at their guest expectantly.

"I'm Rebecca Canon," said their visitor, taking his hand. "I hope I'm not interrupting. I called your daughter and asked if it would be okay if I dropped by to meet you."

"Of course, it is," said Mrs. Bartley. "We are still in shock over the blessing God sent us through you. We can't thank you enough."

"Well, after Valery went out of her way to help an old lady she couldn't have thought could do anything for her, I took the liberty of having my lawyers do some research on her—and you. I hope you don't mind, but I thought it important that you understand."

The Bartleys nodded but said nothing.

"I am fortunate at my age to be living a very comfortable life. But I assure you, it has not always been so. You see,

I too am originally from Clarendon parish." The Bartleys looked at each other in surprise and then back at her.

"Go on," said Mr. Bartley.

"My parents were farmers who rented a small piece of land where they were able to grow just enough food for the family to survive. The only money my father made was from side jobs like cutting grass or painting houses.

"Neither of them could read or write but it was their dream that I would have opportunities they never had. I had few clothes to wear to school, but when I did go, I made good use of the time. Occasionally, my mother washed clothes for the more privileged people in the village. Sometimes they would give her a dress or two that they no longer wanted instead of paying her.

"Then, when I was twelve and just out of primary school, my parents could no longer afford to pay the rent on the property they occupied. You see, the landlord raised the rent because my mother refused to sleep with him. She never told Papa about what the man was doing for fear that he would think she was encouraging him, so she was left to suffer guilt when the family was forced to move.

"But, although I was still very young, she told me. She wanted me to know the kind of world I was growing up in and told me never to allow men to have power over me, no matter what the cost. We moved to another place and, although the plot of land was much smaller, we got by, and we were happy.

"Then, when I turned sixteen, I took a job as a housemaid for a family from England who had been stationed in

Jamaica. The husband was retired from the British Navy, the wife was a retired nurse, and their only child, Monica, became an airline engineer who later left to live here in the USA. The couple saw that I was hardworking, honest, and intelligent—with more potential than to simply work as a housemaid for the rest of my life—and they asked their daughter to help me emigrate to America. It took a few years, as Monica first had to get settled herself in the American way of life, but she sponsored me, and everything fell into place.

"Not long after, I met the love of my life and married him. He worked very hard, working constantly to build the business that gave me this comfortable life." She pulled a photograph from her purse and showed it to the couple.

"He died almost ten years ago now and left the business to me…and my son. I have spent every day since seeking to fill the void his absence left in my life. For fifty years, my husband helped thousands of people to have homes of their own. So, in his honor, it has been my mission these past ten years to help those good people he helped who meet with misfortune to keep theirs. When I found out about your accident, Mr. Bartley, I knew what might happen, and I bought your mortgage.

"But you must understand something else. Without your daughter, who has become quite special to me, I might never have known of your hardship. And if she hadn't held tightly to her vision of you all still living here free and clear of your debts, I might never have followed a whim to go to the grocery store on my own that day. I assure you that I have plenty of staff to take care of the shopping.

"The author Paulo Coelho once said, 'When you want something, the whole universe conspires to make it happen.' The way I see it, the universe—or God, if you prefer—most certainly had a hand in this."

THIRTEEN

The Bartleys' news soon spread through the neighborhood—even to Lambert's mother.

Mrs. DaCosta met her son at the door one afternoon as he returned from school. "Don't you think it's time I met your friend Valery?" she said.

Lambert smiled. "Well, Mommy, Valery's a very spirited young woman, but I'll ask her over for dinner." He did and Valery accepted.

The following Sunday, Lambert escorted Valery to his front door. Mrs. DaCosta, who was waiting just inside, opened the door. "So, this is the lovely girl who has had such a tremendous effect on my son's life!"

Valery looked at Lambert and he shrugged. "I told Mommy all about you. She knows everything."

Valery politely stretched out her hand to Mrs. DaCosta, but Lambert's mother ignored the gesture. "Oh, come on, my dear!" She opened her arms and threw them around the young woman. Valery looked at Lambert again with raised eyebrows, but this time with the hint of a smile.

Finally, Mrs. DaCosta released her. "I'm so happy to meet you, my dear. Lambert thinks the world of you. Tell me, what did you do to my son? What did you say to him?"

Valery thought for a moment. "Well, Mrs. DaCosta, I told Lambert to think of what he wanted—not what he was afraid would or wouldn't happen."

Lambert's mother frowned, trying to understand.

"It's actually very simple," continued Valery, "but it's not always easy. Our thoughts and imagination create feelings, feelings create vibrations, and vibrations align with similar vibrations. Think sad thoughts, feel sad, and you will attract more of the same. If we expect something bad to happen, we feel anxious and afraid, and the things we're anxious about come to pass.

"However, the opposite is also true. If we think of what we want to happen, imagine what we desire to happen, and then expect those things to appear, we will attract those good things. It's all up to us—and our thoughts."

Mrs. DaCosta was so impressed that the next week, she invited the Bartleys and other families to hear Valery and Lambert talk about their experiences.

When everyone had gathered some refreshments and returned to the living room, Valery heard the song of a robin outside the window. When she looked up, it tipped its head and then flew away toward the heavens. Auntie Genie had completed her mission—it was Valery's turn to spread the word.

And now it's yours…

Acknowledgments

Thanks to Jennifer Chin for going above and beyond to make this book a reality;

To Andell Forgie, for your inspiration and guidance;

To my lovely wife Paulette, whom I can call my co-writer, for being there for me with every word, sharing. I love you, my guardian angel.

To Vally Sharpe, my new teacher. Thank you so much for your continuous help. I am happy for this new relationship.

About the Author

Donovan Chin is a Jamaican man who lives in the Bronx, New York. Formerly a model for Nigerian fashion designers, he is also an actor, who played Carl Bullins in the television series "Illegal Aliens," which aired in Jamaica. He also wrote, directed, and produced the movie "Lies and Revelations."

Donovan enjoys gardening, the study of herbs and their benefits, and working out at the gym, but his greatest passion is writing. He hopes that he can communicate something of value to those who read his works.

www.ingramcontent.com/pod-product-compliance
Lightning Source LLC
LaVergne TN
LVHW091120150826
845673LV00002B/904

* 9 7 8 1 9 5 2 2 4 8 5 0 4 *